This book belongs to:

_____

_____

_____

First published 2009 by Walker Books Ltd
87 Vauxhall Walk, London SE11 5HJ

This edition published 2010

10 9

© 2009 Lucy Cousins
Lucy Cousins font © 2009 Lucy Cousins

The author/illustrator has asserted her moral rights.

Illustrated in the style of Lucy Cousins by King Rollo Films Ltd.
Maisy™. Maisy is a registered trademark of Walker Books Ltd, London

Printed in China

British Library Cataloguing in Publication Data:
a catalogue record for this book is
available from the British Library

ISBN 978-1-4063-2559-1

www.walker.co.uk

Maisy Goes to Nursery

Lucy Cousins

WALKER BOOKS

AND SUBSIDIARIES

LONDON • BOSTON • SYDNEY • AUCKLAND

Today was a very good day for Maisy because she went to nursery.

There's always so much to do at nursery, and so many friends to see.

Tallulah   Maisy   Dotty   Cyril

First Maisy hung her coat
on her own special peg
with her name on it.

"Hello, Dotty," she said.
"Hello, Maisy," said Dotty.
"Look, Cyril must be here
too, and Tallulah."

"Good morning, Maisy and Dotty!" said Mr Peacock.

"We are starting with painting today."

What brilliant paintings!
Mr Peacock helped put
them up on the wall.
"That's my new house,"
Maisy said.

"And that's Maisy and me, dancing," said Dotty.

At elevenses, they had drinks, biscuits and fruit.

"Thank you very, very, very much," Tallulah said. "Oh, yummy, scrummy!"

Maisy and Dotty went to the little toilets.

Tallulah reminded them
to wash their
hands.

"Book time!" called Mr Peacock.
"Gather round, everybody."

They all sat together
and listened quietly
to the story.

"Once upon a time..."

Then it was quiet time. Everybody fetched their blankets and snuggled down for a nap.

Then came a noisy time.
Maisy played the guitar.
Dotty played the drums.

Everyone played something and joined in for a sing-song.

Out in the garden,
everyone got busy ...

digging in the
sandpit ...

playing
with a
ball ...

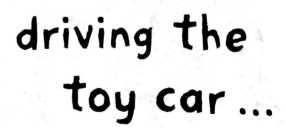

driving the
toy car ...

skipping ...
dancing ...

playing
on the
see-saw.

Oh, how busy they all were, until it was time to go home.

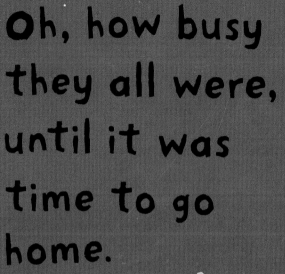

Maisy really likes nursery.

"Goodbye, Dotty. Goodbye, Maisy."
"Goodbye, Mr Peacock."

What a very good day!